All About "A"

How many things in this picture begin with the letter A?

Illustrated by Barbara Gray

Answer on page 47.

INCHING ALONG

Help the inchworms join their friends so they can measure the foot before it runs away. Hurry!

START

START

Illustrated by Pat Merrell

START

FINISH

Answer on page 47.

ANIMAL CRACKERS

Add one letter from the alphabet soup to each word on an animal cracker and rearrange them to spell the name of the animal. For example, ARE + B can be rearranged to spell BEAR. Can you name the rest of the animals?

Illustrated by Jerry Zimmerman

1. ARE
2. MEAL
3. OIL
4. TAG
5. MONEY
6. ROSE

Answer on page 47.

WHO IS IT?

Did someone eat too much lunch? Connect the dots to find out.

I'M STUFFED!

Illustrated by Judith Hunt

Answer on page 47.

SNACK TRACK

Help Tracy track down her picnic snack. Start at her table. Follow the clues. When you find anything outlined in red, write its name on Tracy's table to spell her snack. You will have one extra letter at the end. Place it in the space on Tracy's bowl to find out what she will have for dessert.

1. Go to the table with a watermelon.
2. Move two tables to the right. Find a green vegetable.
3. Go to the table with fried chicken and tossed salad.
4. Move one table to the left.
5. Go to the table with steak and potatoes.
6. Move to the table with marshmallows.
7. Move left one table.
8. Go up to the other table with a hamburger.
9. Eat!

UP
LEFT   RIGHT
DOWN

S _ RAWBERRIES

Tracy's Snack:

_ _ _ _ _ _   _ _ _ _ _

_ _ _ _ _ _ _

TEAM WORDS

Each pair of pictures teams up to make a word. The first one is "notebook." Can you tell what the others are?

1.

2.

3.

4.

5.

6.

Illustrated by Dennis Panek

Answer on page 47.

WIPE OUT!

Someone erased part of the blackboard work. Can you figure out what should be there?

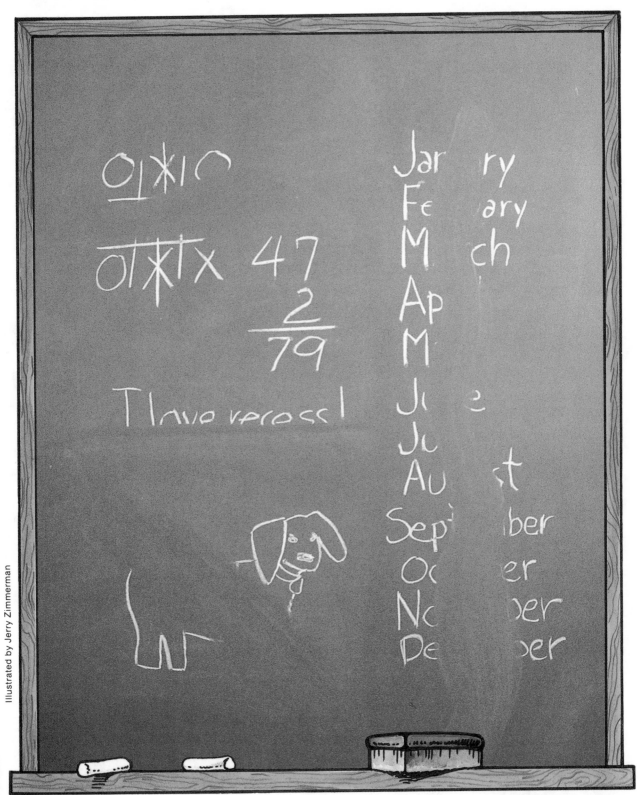

Illustrated by Jerry Zimmerman

TRAVEL TROUBLE

How many things can you find wrong with this picture?

Illustrated by Jerry Zimmerman

ROW, ROW, ROW

Each car has something in common with the two others in the same row. For example, all three cars in the top row across have their tops down. Look at the other rows across, down, and diagonally. What's the same about each row of three?

Illustrated by Paul Richer

Answer on page 47.

RUBY'S TUBE

Help Ruby float safely back to her towel on the beach.

START

FINISH

Answer on page 47.

GRITS IN YOUR GALOSHES

Which would you see if you found . . .

1. . . . grits in your galoshes?

A.  B.

2. . . . a bobolink on your bungalow?

A.  B.

3. . . . a jester in your juniper?

A.  B.

4. . . . okra in your oboe?

A.

B.

5. . . . a gecko on your goblet?

A.

B.

6. . . . a polliwog on your prow?

A.

B.

Answer on page 48.

ONE BY ONE

How many times can you find the word "ONE" in the letters below?
Look up, down, sideways, backward, and diagonally.

```
O N E O E O
N N N N N N
O E O E O E
N N N N N N
E O E O N E
N E N O N E
```

Answer on page 48.

"OA" WE GO!

Every word in this puzzle includes the letters OA. Use the clues across and down to complete the words.

Across
3. Brag
5. Lion's sound
7. Froglike animal
10. Long, heavy jacket
11. Warm, crunchy breakfast bread
12. Sudsy bar for your bath
15. Rowboat's paddle
16. To make very wet
17. Frog's sound
18. Football team boss

Down
1. Billy or Nanny animal
2. Food for a horse
3. Long, flat piece of sawed wood
4. Ship
6. Street or highway
8. Water in the desert
9. Unsliced bread
13. Acorn tree
14. A way to cook eggs

Illustrated by Dennis Panek

A SHIRT SENTENCE

The Puzzle Club has a message to send, but the members' shirts are scrambled. Write the words in order, and make a shirt sentence.

Illustrated by John Ne

CRACKERJOKE

What's the joke?
Crack the code and find out.

A = R	G = U	N = F	U = G
B = Y	H = Q	O = Z	V = I
C = L	I = V	P = X	W = M
D = J	J = D	Q = H	X = P
E = S	K = T	R = A	Y = B
F = N	L = C	S = E	Z = O
	M = W	T = K	

Answer on page 48.

PLAYGROUND PAL

Finish the poem by putting the rhyming words in place.

clap   hop   top   lick   wings
stick   swings   lap   tree   me

If I had a dinosaur
   as tall as a _ _ _ _ _ ,
She'd go to the playground
   with my friends and _ _ .

She'd climb up the jungle gym
   with a tiny _ _ _ _ .
Then I'd climb up on her,
   to the tippy-_ _ _ .

My dinosaur could never
   fit on the _ _ _ _ _ _ ,
But she'd push me so high
   That I'd think I had _ _ _ _ _ .

She'd sit on the slide
   and hold me on her _ _ _ ,
Then she'd zoom to the ground
   while all the kids would _ _ _ _ .

On the way home we'd buy
   ice cream on a _ _ _ _ _ .
My dinosaur would eat it all
   with one little _ _ _ _ .

Illustrated by Pat Merrell

Answer on page 48.

FRANNY'S FAMILY

Franny's family is mixed with a few friends in this picture. Find how many people are in Franny's family by using the clues below.

In Franny's family:

1. Everyone wears boots.
2. Everyone wears green.
3. One person has freckles.
4. Everyone has a watch.
5. Everyone wears glasses.

4.

1.

2.

3.

5.

6.

8.

7.

Answer on page 48.

TOP SPEED

If all the contestants in this race were running at top speed, who would be the fastest? Who would be the slowest? Which animals could the man outrun at top speed?

Answer on page 48.

STOP, LOOK, AND LIST

Under each category list one thing that begins with each letter. One bakery treat that begins with *B* is *bread*. See if you can name another.

Bakery Treats

B_____

D_____

T_____

P_____

C_____

Clothing

B_____

D_____

T_____

P_____

C_____

3-Letter Words

B_____

D_____

T_____

P_____

C_____

Answer on page 48.

Illustrated by Doug Taylor

PICTURE MIXER

Copy these mixed-up squares in the spaces on the next page to put this picture back together. The letters and numbers tell you where each square belongs. The first one, A-3, has been done for you.

A-1	A-2	A-3	A-4
B-1	B-2	B-3	B-4
C-1	C-2	C-3	C-4
D-1	D-2	D-3	D-4

Answer on page 49.

ZOO VIEW

Your helicopter is flying over a zoo.
How many animals do you recognize?

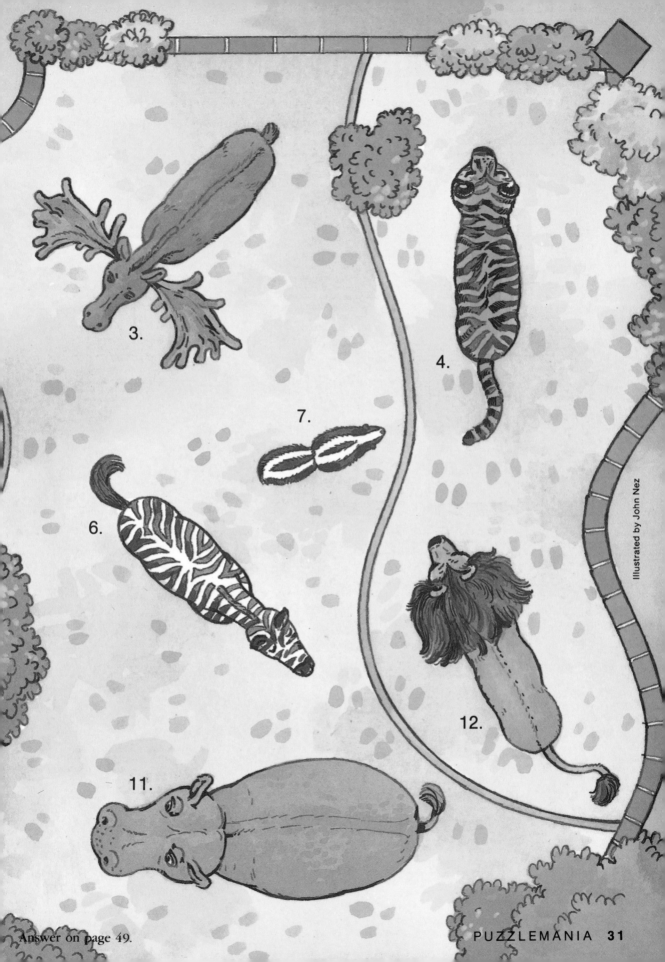

3.

4.

7.

6.

12.

11.

Illustrated by John Nez

MIND YOUR MARBLES!

Where will the blue marble come out?
Where will the red marble come out?

Answer on page 49.

TIME TRAVEL

The time machine just landed, but the travelers are lost in time. Their trip began this year. Here is a chart of their travels. The 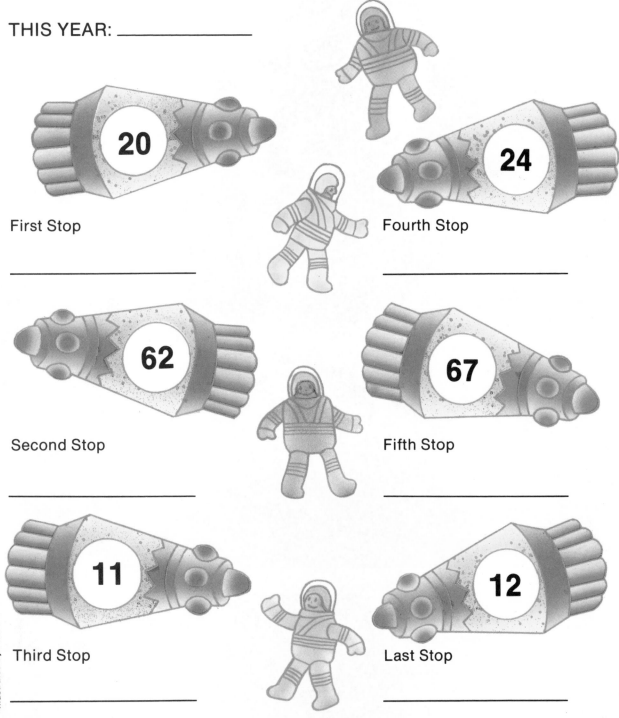 means a trip into the future. Add these years. The means a trip into the past. Subtract these years. Their first stop took them ahead twenty years, so add twenty to the starting date. In what year did they finally land?

THIS YEAR: _____

20

First Stop

_____

62

Second Stop

_____

11

Third Stop

_____

24

Fourth Stop

_____

67

Fifth Stop

_____

12

Last Stop

_____

Answer on page 49.

GUESS WHO!

You like me to come to your pool parties and picnics.
I help you see.
I wake some people up in the morning.
If you spend too much time with me, I may burn you.
I am often the center of attention. The world revolves around me.
Some people have glasses named after me.
I get lost in the clouds.

Who am I?

Answer on page 49.

SINGING BEES

You've heard of spelling bees. These are singing bees. Use the notes on the musical scale to find out what words the bees are singing. The first one has been done for you.

Scale

E F G A B C D

1. **BEE**

2.

3.

4.

5.

6.

7.

8.

HIDDEN PICTURES

How many objects can you find hidden
in this picture?

Illustrated by Joe Boddy

GLENDA'S GOODIES

Use these tasty clues to fill in the yummy words below. Place each cookie letter on a space below to find out where Glenda keeps her goodies.

_ _ _ _ _ _ 1. Frosting

_ _ _ _ _ _ _ _ _ 2. Cookie chip flavor

_ _ _ _ _ _ _ 3. Hot breakfast cereal

_ _ _ _ _ _ _ 4. Cookie factory

_ _ _ _ _ _ _ 5. White ice cream flavor

_ _ _ _ _ _ _ _ 6. After meal treat

_ _ _ _ 7. Peanut butter's partner

_ _ _ _ 8. To cook in the oven

_ _ _ _ _ _ 9. Dried grapes

Glenda keeps her goodies in a:

_ _ _ _ _ _ _   _ _ _ .

Illustrated by John Nez

Answer on page 49.

DIVE IN

Connect the dots to find out what made
a big splash in the pond.

Illustrated by Judith Hunt

TAKE A CLOSE LOOK

There are at least 15 differences between these two views through the microscope. How many can you find?

SEEK AND FIND

Use the pictures as clues and find the words hidden in the letters below. Look up, down, sideways, backward, and diagonally.

```
T R E W O L F W A N
S M G R Y D A Z C S
D Q I M N T B G S M
O F E Z C R L U N I
O S C H D A G I O L
R U L E R E C T O E
N W Z E T H J A L B
F F E L R H E R L F
B R S F O E I J A H
T T O O B Z C L B D
```

Answer on page 49.

BLOCK PARTY

Baby BooBoo put her blocks in a special order. Which one will she put next in line?

Her big brother Todd stacked his blocks in order, too. Which one will he put on top of the tower?

Answer on page 50.

WHO HATCHED?

Who just hatched from this egg? Use your imagination to finish the drawing.

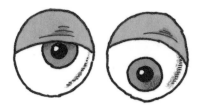

Illustrated by Pat Merrell

THE GAME GANG

Unscramble the letters to spell great games for the whole gang. In each picture, letters of the same color make one word.

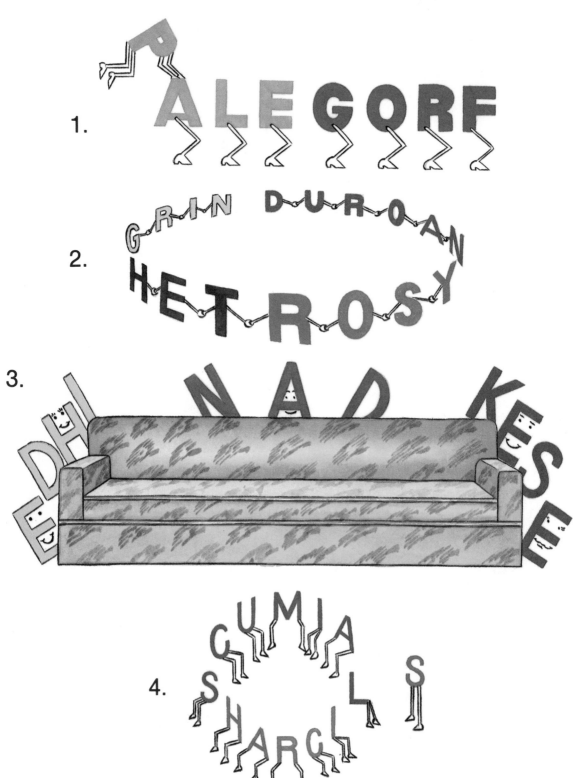

1.

2.

3.

4.

5.

NOLNOD REGBID

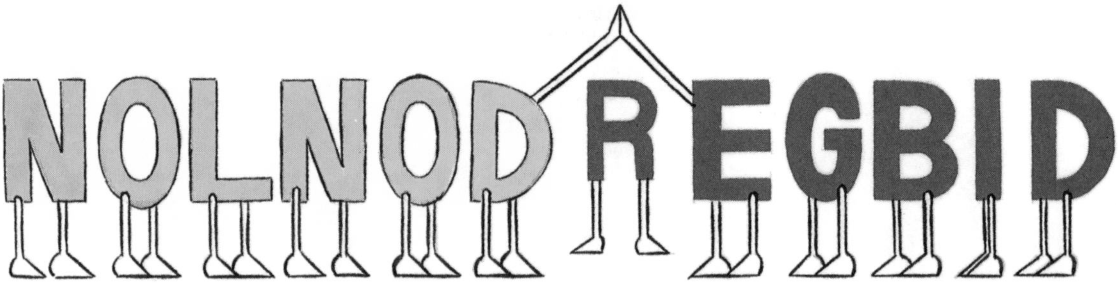

6.

ERD NERG
THILG THILG
E

7.

DER VORRE

8.

KUCD KUCD
O
SOG
E

Illustrated by Jennifer Skopp

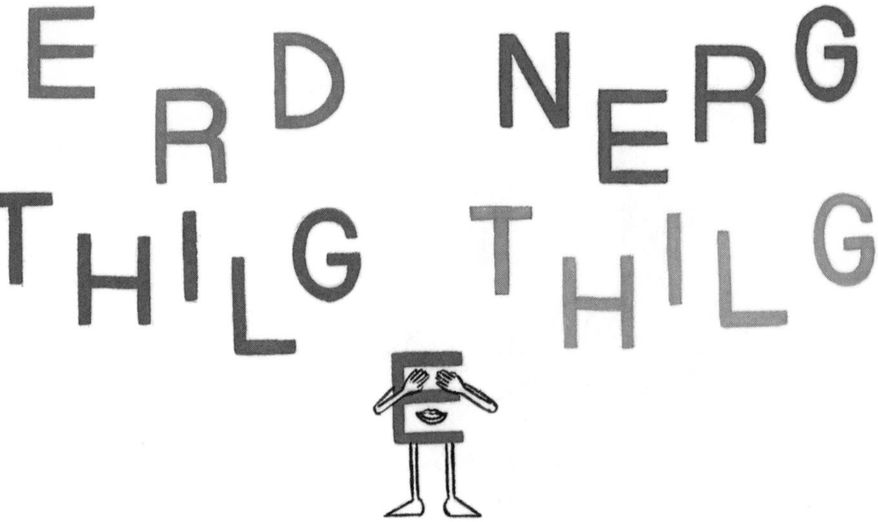

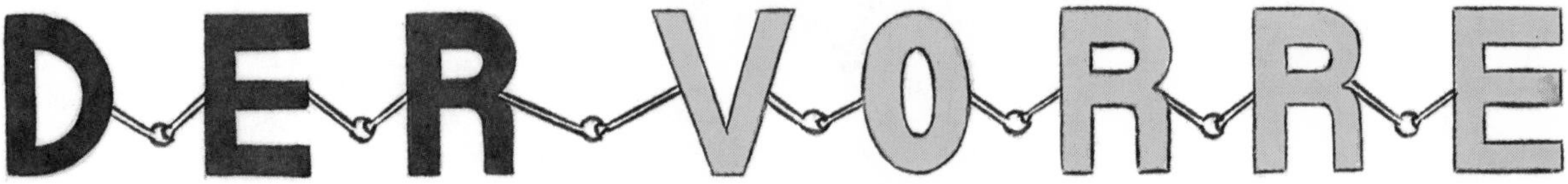

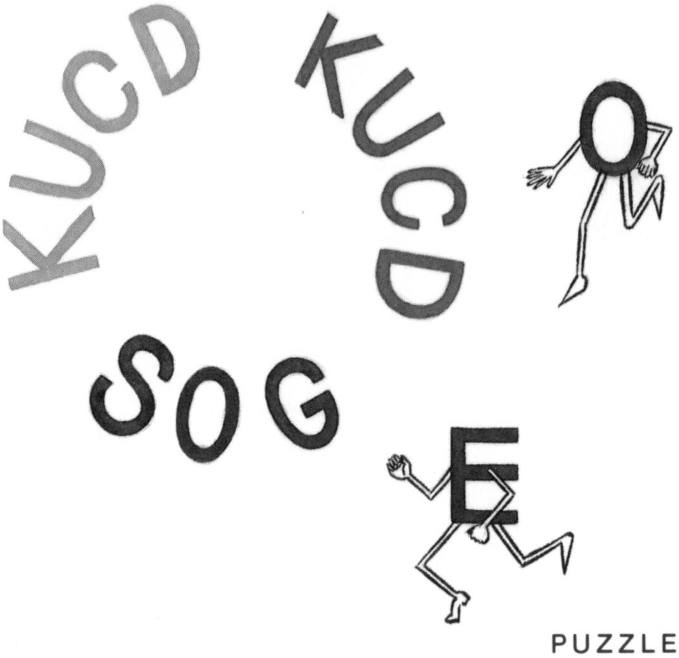

Answer on page 50.

PENCIL PAIR

Only two pencils on this page look exactly alike. Can you find them?

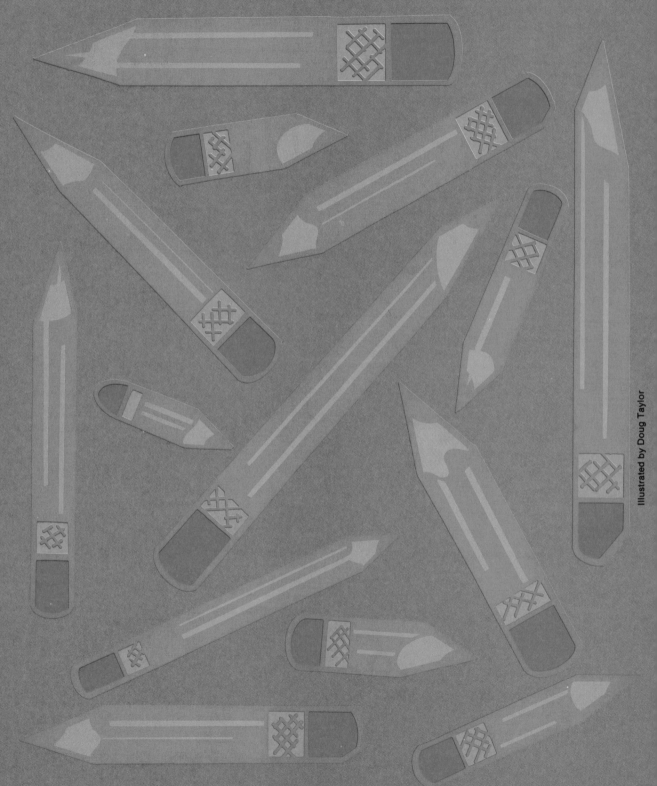

Illustrated by Doug Taylor

Answer on page 50.

ANSWERS

COVER

The matching balls are 2 and 7.

ALL ABOUT "A" (page 3)

accordion	ankle	arch
ace	anteater	arm
acorn	antennae	armor
addition	antlers	arrows
address	ants	art
airplane	ape	artichoke
alien	apples	artist
American flag	apron	astronaut
angle	aquarium	avocado

INCHING ALONG (pages 4-5)

ANIMAL CRACKERS (page 6)

1. Bear
2. Camel
3. Lion
4. Goat
5. Monkey
6. Horse

WHO IS IT? (page 7)

SNACK TRACK (pages 8-9)

Tracy's snack is a peanut butter sandwich. Her dessert is strawberries.

TEAM WORDS (page 10)

1. Notebook
2. Eyeball
3. Tablespoon
4. Watchdog
5. Firecracker
6. Pocketbook

WIPE OUT! (page 11)

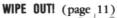

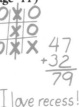

$$47 + 32 = 79$$

I love recess!

January
February
March
April
May
June
July
August
September
October
November
December

ROW, ROW, ROW (page 14)

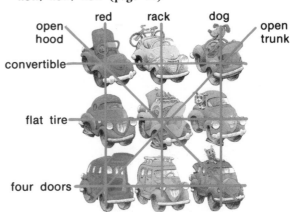

RUBY'S TUBE (page 15)

GRITS IN YOUR GALOSHES (pages 16-17)

1. A
2. B
3. B
4. A
5. A
6. B

ONE BY ONE (page 18)

"ONE" appears twenty-four times.

"OA" WE GO (page 19)

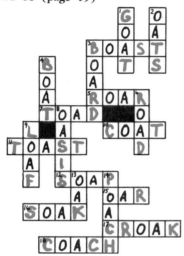

A SHIRT SENTENCE (pages 20-21)

Puzzle people need sharp pencils and sharp minds!

CRACKERJOKE (page 22)

1. Where does Thursday come before Wednesday?
2. In the dictionary.
3. Ha Ha Ha!

PLAYGROUND PAL (page 23)

If I had a dinosaur
   as tall as a *tree*,
She'd go to the playground
   with my friends and *me*.

She'd climb up the jungle gym
   with a tiny *hop*.
Then I'd climb up on her,
   to the tippy-*top*.

My dinosaur could never
   fit on the *swings*,
But she'd push me so high,
   that I'd think I had *wings*.

She'd sit on the slide
   and hold me on her *lap*,
Then she'd zoom to the ground
   while all the kids would *clap*.

On the way home we'd buy
   ice cream on a *stick*.
My dinosaur would eat it all
   with one little *lick*.

FRANNY'S FAMILY (pages 24-25)

Franny's family members include: herself, 4, 5, and 6.

TOP SPEED (page 26)

The cheetah would be the fastest at about 70 miles per hour.
The tortoise would be the slowest at about 2 mph.
The man, at about 25 mph, would outrun the pig (about 10 mph) and the tortoise.
The top speed of the giraffe, dog, kangaroo, and horse are all between 35 and 50 mph.

STOP, LOOK, AND LIST (page 27)

Here are our answers. You may have found others.

Bakery Treats	Clothing
Bread	Belt
Doughnut	Dress
Tart	Tie
Pie	Pants
Cake	Coat

3-Letter Words
Big
Dog
Top
Pan
Cat

PICTURE MIXER (pages 28-29)

ZOO VIEW (pages 30-31)

1. Elephant
2. Giraffe
3. Moose
4. Tiger
5. Kangaroo
6. Zebra
7. Skunk
8. Flamingo
9. Penguin
10. Peacock
11. Hippopotamus
12. Lion

MIND YOUR MARBLES! (page 32)

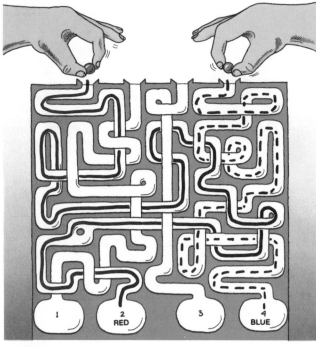

TIME TRAVEL (page 33)

The time travelers finally landed in the same year they began.

GUESS WHO! (page 34)

The Sun

SINGING BEES (page 35)

1. Bee
2. Egg
3. Age
4. Face
5. Edge
6. Bead
7. Decade
8. Cabbage

GLENDA'S GOODIES (page 38)

1. Frosting — ICING
2. Cookie chip flavor — CHOCOLATE
3. Hot breakfast cereal — OATMEAL
4. Cookie factory — BAKERY
5. White ice cream flavor — VANILLA
6. After meal treat — DESSERT
7. Peanut butter's partner — JELLY
8. To cook in the oven — BAKE
9. Dried grapes — RAISINS

Glenda keeps her goodies in a: COOKIE JAR

DIVE IN (page 39)

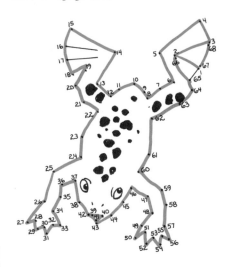

SEEK AND FIND (page 41)

BLOCK PARTY (page 42)

GAME GANG (pages 44-45)

1. Leap Frog
2. Ring Around The Rosy
3. Hide And Seek
4. Musical Chairs
5. London Bridge
6. Red Light, Green Light
7. Red Rover
8. Duck, Duck, Goose

PENCIL PAIR (page 46)